THE WEDDING-DAY
SCRAMBLE

by
ANNE FORSYTH
Illustrated by Kate Rogers

HAMISH HAMILTON
LONDON

The words of the *Lewis Bridal Song* on page 57
are reproduced by kind permission of
Roberton Publications
on behalf of
The Sir Hugh S. Roberton's Trust.

First published in Great Britain 1985
by Hamish Hamilton Children's Books
Garden House   57–59   Long Acre   London WC2E 9JZ
Copyright © 1985 by Anne Forsyth
Illustrations copyright © 1985 by Kate Rogers

British Library Cataloguing in Publication Data
Forsyth, Anne
   The Wedding-Day Scramble—(Antelope books)
   I. Title   II. Rogers, Kate, 1960
   823'.914[J]   PZ7
   ISBN 0–241–11533–7

Filmset in Baskerville by
Katerprint Co. Ltd, Oxford
Printed in Great Britain at the
University Press, Cambridge

Chapter 1

"MY SISTER Mairi's getting married," said Allie when it was news time in class.

There was a buzz of excitement.

Things were a little quiet in Glenfair at the moment. It would be some time till the summer visitors arrived in the little village on the shores of a West Highland loch. It would be a month or two till the rash of Bed and Breakfast signs appeared everywhere.

Allie was rather pleased to be the centre of attraction for once. Usually her news was rather dull compared with the other children's reports. Just a few weeks ago, Morag's aunt had been on a TV quiz show. Then Billy's spaniel had had five pups. And the Macnabs' cat had got stuck up a tree and had to be rescued by the fire brigade.

Nothing half as interesting had happened in Allie's home for a very long time.

But a wedding—that was a bit of excitement.

"It's going to be a big wedding," she went on. She told them all about the plans—the wedding in church, then the reception in the village hall, with a wonderful spread—better than anything Glenfair had ever seen before.

"And you're all invited," said Allie suddenly, looking round the class. "You've all to come to the church and to the hall afterwards."

Everyone cheered very loudly at that, and the teacher said, "Well, that's very good news, but settle down now." As if anyone could settle down to reading and spelling and ordinary everyday things, after such a piece of news!

Still, Allie was right. It was going to be a splendid wedding.

"I want a real old-fashioned wedding—with all the old customs," said Mairi dreamily.

"I want a piper to play us from the church. Oh, and a lucky horseshoe. And something borrowed—something blue, of course. And the men will wear the kilt, and we'll have dancing till midnight.

"I'll have two bridesmaids—grown-up, of course," she added.

Allie didn't mind about that, because she didn't want to be a bridesmaid anyway. She usually hated dressing up—she'd much rather wear jeans and an old jersey.

"And then," Mairi continued, "when we move into our new house, I want Robert to carry me over the threshold and one of you to break an oatcake over my head."

"You'll get your hair full of crumbs," Allie chipped in.

Mairi gave her a crushing look. "It's an old Scottish custom."

Their father groaned and said what would the bridegroom and his family up from England think of all this non-sense?

But Mairi paid no attention. She just went on making plans.

The wedding was to be on the first Saturday in June. It had been a cold wet spring.

People turned up the collars of their coats and wound their scarves round their necks, and scurried out of the biting north wind.

But it was sure to be sunny by the first Saturday in June.

Every day Allie had more news for her class.

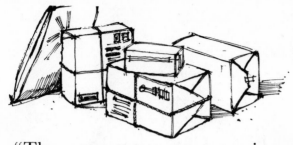

"The presents are coming in already," she told them.

And sure enough they were—in brown paper parcels, in padded envelopes, in large cardboard boxes from Edinburgh.

That very morning the postman had arrived at the door with a parcel which was bursting open already. "This one nearly didn't make it," he said.

"And there's going to be a piper," said Allie importantly. The class all knew the piper. Sandy was the best piper for miles around—hadn't he won all kinds of prizes and played at the Highland Festival too?

He said he'd be honoured to play at the wedding and he'd compose a new tune specially for the occasion.

"And the food . . ." Allie went on. The class all listened eagerly.

Almost everyone in the village was helping—making sausage rolls and other savouries, and storing them in freezers till the great day.

"It's to be help-yourself," Allie told the class. "That means you can eat as much as you want."

No doubt about it—Allie was popular. Everyone wanted to sit beside her and to lend her pencils and notebooks and their favourite comics—just in case she changed her mind about you and decided to cross you off the guest list.

As they walked home, Allie told her best friend, Peg, more about the wedding.

"We're having turkey and roast beef and salmon—and salad. As much as you want."

"And trifle?" Peg had a sweet tooth.

"Trifle and jelly and ice cream—and meringues," said Allie impressively. "And a cake—all covered in pink roses."

Peg was almost as excited as Allie. For one thing, she was a little bored at the moment because her brothers, Dougal and Danny, were extra busy on a project of their own. They didn't want Peg around. And she felt shut out.

Perhaps Dougal and Danny were the only people in Glenfair who weren't interested in the wedding plans. They were busy trying to set up a taxi service. They were determined it would be ready in time for the arrival of the summer visitors.

The taxi was a wooden box on four wheels. They'd begged the box from Mr Macbride, owner of the village general store. Someone had given them the wheels from an old pram. Dougal and Danny spent hours building the cart. Then they painted the wooden box and finally stencilled **TAXI** in large letters on the side.

Peg was very scornful.

"Who's going to go in that!" she said.

They would certainly have to be fairly small, or else sit with their knees hunched up to their chins.

But Dougal and Danny didn't pay any attention to her. They were proud of their taxi. It went very fast—sometimes a bit too fast round the corners.

"And it hasn't got any cover on top," said Peg.

"Well," said Danny reasonably, "in foreign countries you ride in open donkey carts. A taxi doesn't need to have a cover on top."

"But in foreign countries it's sunny," said Peg. "It rains nearly all the time here. People will get very wet."

They didn't pay any attention to her, so she went away, with a scornful look at the taxi.

Chapter Two

Meanwhile, Allie's class were full of plans.

They made collage pictures of the wedding—from bits of shiny paper and pieces of net and lace.

They made models of the wedding feast—model turkey, model cake—from clay.

They learned the Lewis Bridal Song, and they sang it all the time.

No one thought of anything else but the wedding.

And then the blow fell.

Mairi and Mum were finishing the guest list.

"Well, that's it," said Mairi. "And definitely no children at the wedding."

"No children!" Allie was horrified.

Mairi couldn't mean it.

"Definitely no children," repeated Mairi. "Oh, you'll be there, of course, but no others. They only howl through the service or else they're sick at the reception. No children."

"But my friends wouldn't howl or be sick," said Allie indignantly. "Besides," she added, rather desperately, "I've already asked them."

"You've what?"

"I've asked my class—and one or two more."

"How many?" Mairi's voice rose.

"Well," Allie thought for a moment, "there's about twenty-five—or maybe twenty-six." There were quite a lot of children because they came to Glenfair from the villages round about.

"Twenty-six!" Mairi's voice rose to a scream.

"Most of them have never been to a wedding," said Allie pathetically. "And I've asked them already."

"Well, you can just un-ask them," said Mairi. "The very idea!"

This really was a problem. Allie didn't know what to do. How could Mairi be so unkind!

And how could she tell her friends— all twenty-six of them—that they weren't invited after all? That they weren't welcome, and they'd have to stay outside the hall while inside the grown-ups fed on turkey and ham and salad and sausage rolls and trifle and meringues. Oh, no, she couldn't do it.

She had promised they could come to the wedding—and a promise is a promise.

She decided to try Mum.

"Mum—couldn't my friends come to the wedding? They'd be very quiet and they wouldn't be sick—honestly."

"Oh, no," said Mum very firmly. "How could we ask twenty-six children? You should have had more sense." Then, seeing that Allie looked rather downcast, she said kindly, "Well, maybe they could come and watch outside the church. And you could take some of the cake to school."

But that wasn't the same thing—not at all. They were all going to be so disappointed. Allie didn't know how she was going to break the news.

"Will there be different sorts of ice cream?" asked Moira.

"And lemonade?" asked Keith. "With straws?"

"I'm not going to eat anything at all the day before," said Billy who was famous for his appetite. "So I'll be able to eat a lot at the wedding."

"I'll wear my new dress," said Shona. "The one my auntie sent me. And I've to get new sandals for my birthday. I'll wear those too."

How could Allie tell them that there was no point in dressing up or saving their appetites for the great day? She couldn't even tell Peg, because Peg was just as excited as the rest.

When at last her friends found out the truth, she thought gloomily, they would never speak to her again.

Was there anything she could do?

Perhaps, she thought hopefully, she could make Mairi change her mind.

Perhaps she could do something very fine and noble, and then Mairi would be so grateful she would say, "Ask anyone you like to the wedding."

But how? She could rescue Mairi from dreadful danger. But there wasn't any danger in Glenfair.

Besides, she wouldn't really want Mairi to be in great danger. She could be quite nice when she wasn't being bossy and pig-headed.

So Allie decided there was only one thing to do. She would be as helpful as she could during the next few weeks, so that Mairi would wonder how she could have been so unkind. "I don't know how we would ever have managed to cope without you," she could hear Mairi saying. "Ask all your friends to the wedding."

So Allie set about being helpful.

It didn't quite work out that way.

For one thing, the house was already full of relatives—popping in and out for meals, or to help with the preparations or just to see what was happening. If Allie said, "Can I help?" they just told her to run away and play and stay out of the way.

She did mean to be helpful.

But—it started with the veil.

Mairi had been showing off her wedding dress and veil and the rest of her finery to a friend. Now she'd gone along with her friend to the bus stop.

Allie peeped into her sister's room. The clothes lay scattered over the bed and the chair. It did look untidy, she thought.

She'd tidy it up for Mairi. That would be a fine, helpful thing to do.

She picked up the wedding veil and was about to put it away when she thought, "I'll just try it on. Mairi won't mind."

Then she tried on the shoes—white satin with small bows. They were much too big for her, but even the small heels made her look quite tall.

She peered through the mist of net. You could almost pretend you were a ghost.

She'd just walk through to the mirror on the landing and see how she looked. After all, no one would see her.

Next Hallowe'en, Allie thought, she might even dress up as a ghost, or even a banshee.

On the way to the long mirror, she

practised a few howls. "Ooooooh . . . whoooh . . ."

It was a pity that Aunt Sadie was passing through the hall down below. It was a pity that she was on her way from kitchen to dining room, carrying a bowl of beetroot for the salad supper that evening.

It was a pity that she heard the ghostly howl. Though it was a very good howl.

Allie was proud of it.

But Aunt Sadie was startled—so startled that she dropped the bowl of beetroot, and watched, horrified, as the dark purple stain spread over the carpet.

Chapter 3

There was real trouble for Allie over that. Even after she'd replaced the veil and shoes, and tried to explain about Hallowe'en and ghosts, they were still cross.

So she tried very hard to make up for it.

But it wasn't really her fault about the cake.

"Can I help?" she asked Mum.

"You can fetch the tablecloths from the sideboard drawer. They'll need to be washed and starched."

Allie went into the dining-room, but when she saw the wedding cake, she forgot all about the cloths.

There it sat, on the dining-room table, looking very splendid with garlands in white icing and shells and roses in pink icing. The roses looked almost real. For the baker was an artist when it came to icing and marzipan. He could make flowers and leaves so lifelike you would swear they were made of silk and not icing.

He could make petals look as if they were just opening and coming into flower.

How did he do it?

Allie had been helping to make a

28

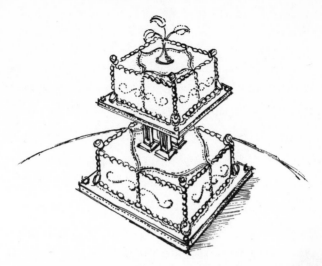

model cake for the display at school. She looked long and hard at the wedding cake. Of course, she thought, it was different with modelling clay.

And then she realised she'd left the door open, and she wasn't the only one looking at the cake. Paddy, the family dog, was hungry. He gazed longingly at the cake. It looked good enough to eat. He was just about to jump up on the dining-room table, when Allie saw him.

"Down, Paddy, down!" she shouted and she cuffed him. It was a pity that her hand caught the roses on the top tier. And it was a pity that one broke off and that Paddy gobbled it up before she could say, "Hey!"

"Oh!" Allie stood, horrified.

And then Mairi came into the dining-room—and stopped.

"Mum! Look at this!" she called dramatically. "Look what she's doing! She's feeding the dog on cake!"

Allie protested loudly. She'd only been looking. She didn't know the dog was there.

Mairi went off in a tantrum and Mum had a few things to say.

After that, Allie was desperately anxious to be helpful. So a few days before the wedding she offered to carry the borrowed plates over to the hall. "See and not break them now," said Mum.

It wasn't really Allie's fault that she was practising being a waitress, carrying two or three along her arm. She didn't notice the stone. She stumbled over it, and four plates went crashing to the ground. "All breakages to be paid for," said Dad gloomily.

"That child is wrecking the wedding already," said Mairi crossly. "Couldn't we send her away until it's all over?"

"She's your own sister," said Mum, trying to smooth things over.

Mairi just groaned.

So did Allie. There was no chance now that Mairi would change her mind. Only a few days to go, and Allie had still to break the news to her friends that they weren't invited.

How was she going to do it?

And then Uncle George came up with his bright idea.

"You'll be having a poor-oot at the wedding?" he said.

"A poor-oot? What's that?" asked Mairi.

"It's an old Scottish custom," said Uncle George. "At a wedding, when the

bridegroom and the best man leave for
the church, all the children gather
round and shout 'poor-oot' and the two
men throw all the pennies in their
pockets—and the children scramble for
them. It's a fine old custom." His eyes
twinkled.

"Poor-oot?" asked Robert, the bridegroom.

He came from England. There were quite a few things in Glenfair that puzzled him.

"Pour-out in English," said Mairi. "You pour the money out of your pockets."

"I remember Granny talking about poor-oots," said Mum.

"And I remember being at a poor-oot when I was a lad," said Dad with a grin. "It was old pennies and ha'pennies in them days, and sometimes

34

thruppeny bits, and once someone threw a sixpence at us."

"Then we'll have a poor-oot," said Mairi. She thought it was a very good idea. "You'll need to stock up with pennies."

"Throwing money away?" said Robert a bit doubtfully.

"It's a bit of fun," said Archie, who was to be the best man. Allie liked him. He was big and cheery and had a hearty sort of laugh.

"I'll tell all my friends about it," she said.

So the next day she announced it to the class. "We're having a different sort of wedding," she said. "Children don't dress up. Because we're having a poor-oot."

"What's a poor-oot?"

35

Allie explained all about it. "It's a scramble—at a wedding. You wear your oldest clothes," she added.

"Like dooking for apples at Hallowe'en?" asked Morag.

"Well, sort of," said Allie.

Shona thought it was a pity about her new dress. But she didn't want to miss the excitement. So she'd just wear jeans and T-shirt like everyone else. It would be a shame to miss the scramble.

"Anyway," said Allie, "we all go along to Archie's house about half an hour before they leave. Then we shout 'poor-oot, poor-oot', till they throw us the money and then we scramble for it."

Everyone thought this was a very good idea.

Robert, the bridegroom, was to stay

with Archie, the best man, and his parents at their cottage, about a mile or so outside the village. Certainly it was quite a way from the church—but worth it, especially if they were to be throwing money away.

"And then you can go and watch the wedding," said Allie rather hesitantly.

"We'll be ready for the feast by then," said Billy with a grin.

"Er—yes," said Allie. How on earth was she going to break the news to her friends?

Chapter 4

The great day arrived. After weeks of rain, the sun had struggled through, and there was no wind to catch at Mairi's veil or to whisk off the guests' hats.

All morning, at Allie's house, people had been coming and going. Mum hardly knew whether she was on her head or her heels.

About an hour before the wedding,

she caught sight of Allie, still wearing her jeans and T-shirt.

"Time you were getting dressed."

The new checked dress and white frilly blouse, with polished sandals and white socks, lay ready.

"But I'm going to the poor-oot," said Allie.

"Not in your new dress." Mum knew what was what. "I never heard such a thing."

"Oh, no. I'll come back to get dressed." Allie had it all very carefully worked out. If she went to the poor-oot on her bike, she could join in the scramble.

Then she'd rush back. She would have nearly twenty minutes to change and to hurry round to the church.

She wasn't going to miss the poor-oot. Not for anything.

"Well, see and be back in time." Mum had a lot of other things to think about. The flowers hadn't arrived yet,

and had she ordered enough milk? And
what about the two cousins who had
quarrelled that morning and still
weren't speaking? And there in the
midst of all the bustle was Mairi. She
sat dreamily stitching a long golden
hair into her wedding dress, because
she thought it would bring her luck.

"We leave sharp at quarter to two," said Mum.

"I'll be back." Allie didn't want to waste any time. She jumped on to her bike and pedalled off to the poor-oot.

From all over the village, children were setting out towards Archie's cottage.

Some of them had come quite a distance on their bikes. Others walked—or ran. There was even a baby brother in a push-chair. No one wanted to be left out.

Just as the first children arrived at the gate of the cottage, old Murdo drew up in his taxi to collect Robert and Archie.

Murdo's taxi had once been a real taxi in Glasgow. Now it was used to carry all sorts of loads—sacks of logs and pieces of machinery as well as people. So it was usually fairly dirty.

But today it looked clean and shining, the inside brushed and spruce, the outside gleaming with polish.

44

And old Murdo looked different too.
He wore his best black suit and he'd
cleaned his boots and stuck a rose in his
buttonhole. Normally, he looked very
grumpy and bad-tempered, often
shouting at the children to get out of his
way. But today, just for the wedding, he
was wearing a huge smile that made
him look quite unlike himself.

When Robert and Archie came out of the cottage, he leapt out of the driving seat where he'd been sitting smoking his pipe, and opened the doors of the taxi as if it was a Rolls-Royce.

Robert and Archie didn't look a bit like their everyday selves either. Both wore new suits and Robert had a red carnation in his buttonhole and Archie a white one. A great cheer went up from the waiting children when the two appeared.

"Here's the bairns!" said Archie.

"My, have I got to pay all this lot?" said Robert, fishing in his pockets.

"Come on!" Allie cried, and they all surged forward, shouting "Poor-oot, poor-oot!"

Old Murdo became his everyday self. "Keep off my paintwork, you wee devils," he shouted. "That's been polished specially. Come on," he called to Robert and Archie. "Let's be on our way."

So he hustled Robert and Archie into the back of the taxi.

"Poor-oot! Poor-oot!" the chant grew louder.

Surely they weren't going to leave without throwing the pennies!

Then Robert wound down the window on his side. "Here!" He flung a fistful of coins.

There were shrieks as the children scrambled, and a piercing wail as someone's fingers got stepped on in the rush.

"Here's some more!" Archie flung out a few pennies and twopenny pieces from his side.

"Let's be off." Old Murdo switched on the engine.

"That's your lot!" shouted Robert.

"Look! Billy's got five p!" Sure enough, Billy, as slippery as an eel, and smaller than the rest, had dodged in among the feet and grabbed a five pence piece.

They all screamed at him.

Archie laughed loudly. "That'll keep them happy. Just a sec—I've a few more coins here." He fumbled in an inside pocket. The taxi was already moving off as he leant out of the win-

dow and threw a handful of coins right at Allie's feet.

"Good luck!" she shouted. There wasn't a scramble this time. All the other children were too busy chasing after Billy.

The coins had rolled to the side of the road. Allie ran to pick them up. There was a penny, a twopenny piece, a couple of old halfpence, a button and— Allie could hardly believe her eyes.

She looked again.

Among the coins was a gold wedding ring.

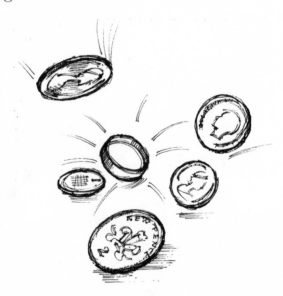

The ring! Mairi's wedding ring. The ring that Archie was supposed to keep safe until he handed it to Robert and Robert put it on Mairi's finger.

Allie picked it up and shouted after the taxi. "Come back! Hey! Come back!"

But the taxi was already disappearing into the distance. It was no use. They couldn't hear her.

Chapter 5

There wasn't a moment to lose. Allie didn't stop to explain to the others. She popped the precious ring into her pocket and jumped on to her bike.

"Can't stop, can't stop!" she called out to the others. They weren't paying any attention to her—they were all busy counting their share of the money.

If she pedalled very hard, she thought desperately, she might just be able to catch the taxi before it reached the church.

Down the hill, round by the farm, the chickens scattered and squawked indignantly as she careered through their midst.

She turned the corner and there, coming out of a gate, was a flock of sheep. They scattered all over the road, a black and white collie barking wildly behind them.

Allie braked and waited, dancing up and down with impatience. The flock meandered from one side of the road to the other. After a moment, the shepherd appeared from the field, closing the gate carefully behind him.

He whistled to the dog. "Good lass, Nell!" And nodded to Allie. "Fine day."

The sheep were still running in all directions. "Oh, hurry, hurry," said Allie to herself.

"Aye, she's a fine pup," said the shepherd with a nod towards the black and white collie. "But young yet, of course. Not used to the work. She'll learn."

At last the dog managed to gather the sheep together and they set off up the road.

Allie got on to her bike again. But

only for a moment or two. Something was wrong. She jumped off the bike and looked at it carefully.

A puncture! She must have ridden over a nail or a sharp stone.

A fine time for this to happen!

There was no time to mend the puncture now. She'd just have to run the rest of the way. A good thing she knew quite a few short cuts to the village.

She kicked the bike crossly.

She took a deep breath and checked in her pocket that the precious ring was still there. Then she set off as fast as she could.

She hummed to herself the Lewis Bridal Song they'd learned at school, remembering the words:

"Step we gaily, on we go,
Heel for heel and toe for toe,
Arm in arm and row on row,
All for Mairi's wedding."

At the end of the road was a group of farm cottages. A young woman was standing at her door, looking up and down the road. As Allie drew nearer, she called, "Are you going to Glenfair?"

Allie nodded, saving her breath.

"Will you do a message for me?"

"I can't," Allie puffed. "I'm in an awful hurry. Got to get to a wedding."

The woman laughed heartily. "Och, you're an awful wee blether. You'll not be going to a wedding dressed like that. Come away in. This'll not take you a minute."

Allie nearly screamed, *"It's true."*

But the woman was already indoors. Allie followed her in.

A small boy was lying on the sofa. He was covered in blankets and looked hot and cross. He gazed at Allie above the bedclothes.

"He's not well," said the woman. "The doctor's been to see him. He left a prescription. Will you take it to the chemist for me? My husband can collect it tonight."

"All right," said Allie, jigging up and down. "But I'm in a terrible hurry, really I am."

The woman took no notice. "Sit down a minute while I get the prescription. I'll not be long."

"I can't sit down!" Allie almost shouted. But still the woman took no notice.

"Now, where did I put it?" she wondered aloud. "It's not in my purse. Oh, maybe it's behind the clock. No, it's not there. Now, that's a mystery. Where can it have got to?"

"I don't know." Allie began edging towards the door.

The small boy began to whine. "Mam, I want a biscuit."

"You be quiet." The woman started to hunt behind the sofa cushions. "No,

it's not here. That's a real puzzle. Maybe it's in the kitchen."

By now the small boy was wailing loudly. Allie felt like joining in.

"Here it is!" the woman called triumphantly. "On the kitchen table all the time."

Allie grabbed the paper out of her hand and rushed towards the door. Down the path, out of the gate, she ran as fast as she could.

"It's all right," the woman called after her. "You don't need to hurry. He's not that seriously ill."

But Allie gritted her teeth and rushed on.

She had never been to a wedding before. When did they put the ring on the bride's finger? At the beginning? Or half-way through? She hoped very much that it was somewhere near the end of the service. Then she might just get there in time.

She had to stop for a minute. She had a stitch in her side. Oh dear, she'd never get there now. Bent double, she thought fast.

A short cut—that was it. If she turned off, round the edge of the next field, then into the little glen beyond, she could cross the bridge over the

burn. Then up the bank, round the next field, and out at the cross roads. She might just be in time.

She took a deep breath. The stitch had gone. "Step we gaily, on we go," she muttered to herself, and started jogging down the road again.

In spring the little glen was carpeted with snowdrops and then with wild

daffodils. But now, under the beech trees, it was wet and soggy. It had rained for weeks, Allie remembered.

She slid down the bank towards the bridge, grasping at roots and tufts of grass. Down, towards the little wooden bridge across the burn.

Except that the bridge wasn't there.

There were only a few wooden struts to show where it had been. The rotting timbers had been wrenched off by the high winds and swept away downstream.

Allie groaned. "Oh, no."

She looked across at the bank on the other side. It was much too far to jump. She thought quickly. There was nothing else for it. She sat down on a log and took off her shoes and socks.

She stuffed the socks inside the shoes and waded rather gingerly into the muddy water.

It wasn't very deep just here, but it was very cold. Carefully, she made her way to the other side, grasped at an overhanging branch, and pulled herself up.

She scrambled up the bank and then sat down to put on her shoes and socks.

By this time, she was wet and very muddy. But there was no time to lose.

She started to run again, round the edge of the field, out of the gate, and there she was, as planned, at the cross roads.

Allie felt very pleased with herself. It had worked out after all.

There was hardly anyone to be seen—they must all be at the church, she thought. She began to run along the road. And then, she saw sitting right in the middle of the road, a large, fluffy black cat.

"Oh, that's lucky," she said to herself.

And then—"Oh, that's Lucky." And she sighed. Because Lucky belonged to an old lady at the other end of the village.

He was large and fat and comfortable, and hardly ever wandered from home. Except this time—and he had been missing for days.

His owner had asked everyone to look out for him.

She'd put a notice in the post office window: "LOST—BLACK, FLUFFY CAT. ANSWERS TO LUCKY". But he still hadn't turned up.

And now here he was, sleek and fat

and very pleased with life. He'd obviously spent the time hunting round the fields.

Allie thought, she couldn't leave him there, now that she'd found him.

"Shoo! Go home, Lucky."

But the cat just sat and blinked at her. So she picked him up and tucked him under her arm.

He didn't like it a bit. He fought and scratched and miaowed loudly.

"You are ungrateful," she told him, but she wouldn't let him go.

When she got to the old lady's house, Lucky's owner was in the front garden.

"Brought him back," panted Allie, thrusting Lucky at her. "Found at cross roads."

The old lady was overjoyed. "Oh,

thank you, thank you," she said as Allie gasped out the story of how she'd found the cat. "Come in, my dear, and have some lemonade and a bite to eat."

Allie drew a deep breath.

"Sister's wedding—poor-oot—pennies thrown—ring too—must get to church—sheep on road—then puncture—wee boy not well—take prescription—short cut—bridge not there—waded through burn—round field—cross roads—found Lucky—off to wedding—can't stop."

"Well, fancy that!" The old lady, with the cat in her arms, stood gazing at the figure that was disappearing into the distance.

"I'll never get there, never get there," Allie panted.

She was quite exhausted by now and

she stopped and leant against a wall.

It was nearly too late. If she hadn't stopped for the sheep, or had a puncture, or met the woman at the cottage, or wasted time crossing the burn, or found the cat and taken it home, then she might just have been in time.

Still, there was nothing she could do about it now.

She started to trudge wearily along the road and then suddenly round the corner, rattling and squeaking came Peg's brothers, Dougal and Danny, with their cart on four wheels which they called the taxi service.

"Hi!" called Allie.

They screeched to a halt.

"Poor-oot-lots—pennies thrown—ring —must get to church—" she stopped to gasp for breath.

"Jump in," said Danny.

So she jumped into the wooden cart and Danny leapt on to the back of it, and Dougal gave it a push and off it went, sailing down the road.

Chapter 6

Down the road, along past the school and Mr Macbride's general store and the chemist and the post office. Danny was good with his hands—he'd fitted an old horn to the front of the cart, and as they rattled past the post office, they hooted loudly.

An old man waved his stick at them. "These laddies! They'll land in the jail," he said gloomily.

Once on the level, Dougal and Danny pulled the cart by ropes. Meanwhile, Allie sat, her knees drawn up to her chin, as pleased as anything. This was better than old Murdo's taxi any day.

On they went round the corner, and stopped right by the church.

By now, all the children had arrived to watch the wedding. Allie climbed out of the cart, nodding graciously. There was Peg and Shona and Morag and Keith and Katrina—oh, and Billy with his five pence piece. They all cheered and she waved her hand as if she were a princess.

Old Murdo's taxi was there too. Dougal and Danny parked right behind him. "Like a taxi rank," said Dougal proudly.

Old Murdo just glared at them. He was his usual self again.

And oh, what a bit of luck—there was no sign yet of Allie's mum, or the bridesmaids, or thank goodness, of Mairi and Dad.

"They're late," Allie heard someone say.

"Just like Mairi."

Well, that was a good thing, thought Allie, as she hurried into the church.

The usher at the door looked very surprised when he saw her.

"Bride's sister," Allie explained.

"I know fine who you are," he said. "You'll not be coming into the church like that."

"I've got to." Allie's voice rose.

Inside the church there was the sound of organ music and the murmur of voices. Heads in flowery summer hats turned towards the door. Voices tut-tutted.

"Did you ever see the like?"

"Fancy her mother letting her out like that."

Allie knew they were talking about her. She felt her face going red.

The usher tried to show her into a back pew. But Allie ignored him. She squared her shoulders and marched down the side of the church, right to the front.

Robert and Archie were standing there, trying to look very calm and cool. But Robert especially was getting more nervous all the time. Where was Mairi? Couldn't she be on time, just for once?

And what was all that row at the back? He wished he could turn round and see.

And another thing—his new shoes were hurting him.

Allie slid into a front pew.

"Hist—hist . . ." She hissed at Archie. Would he never turn round?

"Hist—Archie!"

And then he turned. And his jaw dropped open when he saw Allie. Certainly she did look very strange. She was covered in mud and brambles. Her hair stood on end and her jeans were torn.

"Get that lassie out of here," said the chief usher to one of the others. "Her mother will have a fit when she gets here."

Perhaps it was lucky that Allie's mum was coping with a last-minute panic at home and had no idea what was going on in the church.

Allie fumbled in the pocket of her jeans. "The ring!" she whispered urgently to Archie. "You threw it away by mistake."

She could just see Archie gulp as he grasped her hand and took the ring from her. There wasn't time to say anything because at that very moment, the organist struck up, "Here comes the bride", and Allie slipped away to the back of the church.

And then there was Mairi coming up the aisle, all white lace and taffeta and her veil over her face so that she couldn't see much through its folds— and perhaps just as well.

After that, everything went smoothly. And at last, the piper launched into the new tune he'd composed specially for the occasion and the wedding party came out of the church and posed for photographs.

Allie watched proudly as Mairi showed off the new gold ring on the third finger of her left hand.

And then Archie appeared. He was very grateful to Allie. He didn't exactly say, "I'll give you half my kingdom", but Allie knew that was more or less what he meant.

So while the photographer was click-

ing away and the guests were *oohing* and *aahing* and pelting Mairi with confetti, Allie and Archie came to a very satisfactory arrangement.

"You see," said Allie, "I promised. And a promise is a promise."

"Leave it to me." Archie didn't waste words. He was a man of action.

So off he went. A quick word with Allie's mum, who saw Allie for the first time. She gasped, and clutched at the railings for support. And then she laughed and nodded and smiled.

Which is how all the children in Allie's class—and a few more besides—came to line up at the back door of the hall. Inside, the reception had begun—you could hear the fiddles tuning up.

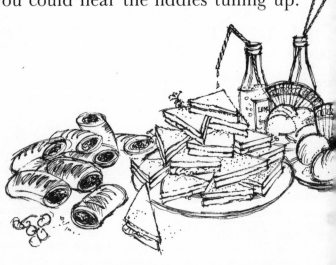

First, the children were given bags of sausage rolls and sandwiches. And after that there were plates of ice cream and trifle and jelly. Maybe it was all a bit mixed up but it tasted fine anyway.

Then bottles of lemonade—and straws—were handed out.

And finally, there was a big plate with pieces of the pink and white wedding cake.

It was a splendid feast. When they'd

finished, even Billy sighed and said he couldn't manage to eat another thing.

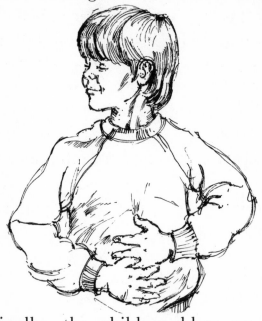

Finally, the children blew up the paper bags and burst them. It was a very fine ending to the day—especially as they all had a few pence from the poor-oot as well.

When Allie had delivered the prescription to the chemist and had rescued her bike and mended the puncture, she went to see Peg. They sat down and shared the last of their pieces of marzipan and icing.

Allie told her friend the whole story right from the beginning, all about the sheep on the road and the puncture, and the woman in the cottage, and crossing the burn, and finding the cat and finally getting there just in time—thanks to Dougal and Danny's taxi service.

And Peg listened and said, "Well!" and "Fancy that!"

And she said she was really sorry she'd said all those horrible things about Dougal and Danny's taxi. Because it had turned out to be a good idea really.

"And what's more," said Allie, "I got into the wedding photos."

She did too. She was right at the end of the row. She had brambles and sticky burrs in her hair, a tear in the leg of her jeans, and mud all over her face—a face that wore a very broad smile.